HOOFS

AN EXTREME STORY

JASON MYERS

CLOVER PEAK PUBLISHING

Hoofs copyright © 2024 by Jason Myers/Clover Peak Publishing

Formatting and cover for this edition by Ruth Anna Evans

First edition 2024

Jason Myers

Clover Peak Publishing

To Lucky,

143.

Dad

"Yeah, that's going to swell for sure. Probably end up with a black eye, too." I said to my son Lucas as sympathetically as I could. I was walking with no more pep in my step than usual as it was his own stubborn fault for showing off. I chuckled to myself as I thought about making a smart assed dad joke to add insult to injury. *That's using your head. Should have zigged, not zagged.* I instead chose to let the boy have this moment of pain and spring into rescue mode.

"Ice pack's in the freezer. I'll grab it while you park it in that chair." I pointed to the dining room table visible through the sliding glass door that accessed the backyard. I put my arm around his shoulders and noticed the calmness in them. I had expected them to be rising and falling uncontrollably in succession with the sobbing and crying that is known to come to even the toughest of backyard football players in all of the neighborhoods in the land.

I looked down and finally cracked a little joke to my son. "Lucas. It's a good thing we named you that. It damn sure shouldn't be Lucky. Bad Lucky, maybe." He stopped, mid step on the stairs that lead up the deck.

My son, the spitting image of his old man, looked up slightly to me and said, "If you would have named me Lucky and not Lucas, you would be the one with the black eye not me." Almost the spitting image of his dad, Lucas broke his poker face and began laughing in a matter of three seconds.

"Almost had me believing you there," I teased. "Better work on that not-breaking character." Both laughing, we pressed on into the house. "You, there." Pointing again to the wooden chair closest to the door. I walked to the refrigerator in the kitchen past the dining room and opened the top freezer. Looking for that never accessible reusable ice pack that I had snagged from one hospital trip or another and coming up empty, I resorted to the old standby. Frozen vegetable medley.

I leaned backward as I held onto the handle of the freezer door and began shuffling around the various things stacked in the way—methodically and very tetris-like—trying to take down the wall of frozen waffles and pancakes trying to get to the veggies that were certain to be long since expired. "Hey, did I ever tell you about the worst black eyes I ever had?"

"Black eyes? As in plural?" Lucas shouted back.

Lego out of my damn way I commanded in my head, sliding the brick that was a yellow box of chocolate-chip waffles out of the picture and was able to free the white, plain as ever, generic branded, plastic vegetable medley. As I lifted it up, "Jackpot," audibly this time. Frozen peas. A drop of the veggies and a snag of the peas and it was off to play "distract the pain by being a storyteller." A game I had mastered long before my son took a perfect spiral thrown football to the left eye.

"Eyes," I handed him the peas and added, "No idea where the ice pack is. Deal with it." I already knew that—even with pain in his eye— the mouth on my kid was going to say something smart back to me about not knowing the difference between peas and ice. "Before you put that on, let me take a peek."

Lucas leaned his head on the hard chair back and I turned the chandelier on to examine the damage the football had done. He was squinting and all it was doing was making his eyelid flutter and distract me from seeing much. "Just relax, I'm not going to touch your eye, I'm just looking." I reassured my nervous child.

"Just like you weren't going to whip a football at me in the backyard?"

And there was the smart-ass he was quickly growing into. "Well maybe I wouldn't have pegged you with it if you weren't trying to catch every damn ball with one hand. I checked, Bud, there weren't any pro scouts out there watching from the trees with binoculars. Jackass. The Lord blessed you with two hands and clearly your mother's athletic ability. Use them both the best you can." I laughed as I leaned out of his face and stood up, noticing the big smile on his. Knowing that this banter was one of countless conversations we had and still to be had is one of my favorite things about being a dad. The give and take and take and give. Clever talks with my children. "Put the bag on there and hold it."

"Black eyes, Dad. On with it."

"Stand up. Let's go sit in the living room and get comfy," I instructed nicely. "Let me regale you with the story of how I got the worst black eyes." a hard emphasis added to "eyes". I reached out to him, still in football-dad mode, and helped him to his feet. Lucas was eleven and one of the quickest-witted kids anyone would meet. A gigantic ego and undeserved sense that he was the biggest person in the room or on the football field, Lucas was the runt of my litter of kids and I knew he loved the fact that "everyone loves the runt" because he was always lightning fast to remind me when I teased him about his stature.

He plopped more than sat on the loveseat that sat underneath the living room's windows and I made a "what are you doing" motion with my hands. That was all it took for him to know to *sit* on the couch, not just crash onto them like a giant sack of potatoes. "Sorry," he said quietly and shifted into a more civilized sitting position and leaned his head back on the couch cushions—peas never leaving the left side of his face.

I walked back to the kitchen and poured a cup of coffee from the pot and then sat on the couch on the wall kitty-cornered from Lucas and the loveseat he was on. I began sitting down and stopped just as quickly in motion as he had just done a few minutes ago on the steps of the deck. "Psst. Watch this." Lucas leaned his head forward off the cushions and I slowly sat down like it was being filmed for a "How to sit on a couch correctly" documentary for television. Lucas leaned right back into the cushions and said, "Yeah, yeah, yeah. Eyes."

I took a sip of the coffee and scoffed, "Eyes. Nah. Eyes were the least of my worries. Hoofs. Now that's where this story starts. Hoofs."

"I had to have been like twenty-five, maybe twenty-six," I began and Lucas shifted for the last time, preparing himself for another Dad-Tale, and being stuck with a frozen plastic bag of peas on his left eye to add to it. "Call it twenty-five. Whatever. I had this piece of junk Pontiac that I drove the hell out of, like it was to be a trusted piece of machinery. The girl I was dating at the time, she lived out about twenty miles past where you live with your mom. Out there in corn country."

"I will never forget the song that was on when the passenger window shattered into my car and the biggest damn deer I have ever seen came crashing through it." I paused and looked to see if I had Lucas's attention. He sat up straight and used his hand to hold the bag onto his eye and used his left hand instead. Safe to say—I had his attention.

"Want to guess the song?" I asked and laughed. I didn't give him a chance to answer and continued on. "I shit you not, Son, that deer came barreling at full speed from this little patch of field between the rows of corn out there in No-Man's Land like a running back and leaped into my stupid Pontiac the minute Axl screamed "Do you know where you are? You're in the jungle, Baby," *Bam*, I clapped my hands together violently once and Lucas was startled. Shot taken. Shot landed.

"This stupid deer was sprinting and timed it out perfectly to obliterate my passenger window, and there I sat, unsuspectingly jamming to Guns N' Roses, smoking a cigarette with *my* —" I tapped myself on my chest at the word "—window rolled down. I went to slam the brakes with my right foot but, for reasons I didn't care about right that particular second, it wouldn't budge. In a split-second I used my left foot that was still free moving and pressed that brake pedal like I was trying to put it through the floor. I told you earlier that the girl I was visiting lived in the country and thank God for that. There was never any traffic."

I stopped myself and tilted my head to the right just a touch and added, "Vehicle traffic,

I should specify," I returned my head from the tilt and said, "Plenty of animals though, apparently." A smile flashed across Lucas's half covered face and I knew then that I had him hooked.

"I bashed that brake pedal and tried to raise my arms up just in case I was going to crash into something. Everyone always says that when they get in car wrecks or near-wrecks that time seems to slow down. Everything slows to a crawl and happens as if in slow-motion. I call bullshit on that one. One second I was cruising. Next second, there was a full grown buck laying across the inside of my car. His big stupid antlers smashed the window and kept on going right across my lap and got stuck with his face half in/half out of my car while it was twisting back and forth trying to free itself."

The speed and intensity of my performance from the couch to an audience of one was picking up and Lucas flipped the bag of peas over in his hand and just before reapplying it like the other side of a pillow, I saw a dark patch definitely forming underneath his swollen shut left eye. I asked him if he was okay and he nodded. Onward I progressed.

"So this giant beast is laying on top of me. That much I can tell. A deer. On me. Shaking like an asshole and surely scratching my shitty car to hell. This is like three whole seconds after it all happened, mind you," I pleaded to my son. "Axl Rose screaming. Glass all over the place. Deer through one window, half out the other. Right leg, pinned down. Car screeching to a stop on the country road and turning hard to the right because of the deer on the steering wheel. And when the clock ticked off to somewhere around second number five, a gigantic deer hoof began its barrage of punches into my face. Only to be followed up by its mate and in a one-two, one-two combo stuck on repeat."

"Every time I would try to raise my arms to block these hoofs-of-fury," I made a reference that, sadly, my son and his entire generation wouldn't catch, "And sometimes my left arm would budge a little bit more and more but my right arm was pretty much useless. My right hand was trapped under the weight of this panicking animal and the most I could get it to move was just enough to wiggle it up and down my thigh by just a couple of inches. Useless to me."

Lucas was scootching up the loveseat's cushion and stopped leaning against the backrest. Full attention and almost worry as I retold the story of being beaten mercilessly at the hands—neh hoofs— of a scared deer when I, myself, was an even more terrified twenty something just trying to get to his girlfriend's house. "What'd you do, Dad?"

"You sure you want to know?" I asked playfully.

"You know I want to know," he belted back at me. "Hoofs. Black eyes. Go."

I smiled and continued on. "Yes sir. Yes sir. So this deer is just beating the ever loving piss out of my face. Only my left hand is free. I keep trying to block all these punches." I paused again and asked Lucas, "Punches? Is that the correct word? Can a deer punch?" Lucas didn't answer out loud, only shrug-

17

ging his shoulders stating that he had no idea.

I was sitting on my own couch, faux blocking an imaginary deer attack while sitting in an imaginary car. Full blown storytelling mode, Lucas was following every word as fast as I was saying them. A passer by power-walking at that exact moment surely would have been laughing at my feeble one arm blocking demonstration looking more like a one arm windshield wiper to the unbeknownst viewer. There was no time to worry about fake sidewalk pedestrians. I muscled on.

"That deer was thrashing and really just fucking up," making sure to muffle my voice by placing my hand partially over my lips and saying the 'ultimate swear word' — according to him anyway—under breath,

18

"Not only my face with its hoofs, but also my drivers door with its antlers. Scratching and making these god awful noises and the whole time it kept beating my face in. Its left hoof into my right eye. Its right hoof into my nose. Left hoof, nose, Right hoof, my mouth." I scootched as my son had done to the edge of my seat and said, "Axl was wrong. I wasn't in the jungle, baby. I was in the corn fields. And I was getting the shit hoofed out of me and was scared to death."

"That's funny Dad," Lucas chuckled. He shifted to his left and right a few times in his best Axl move. Another win in the Dad column. The kid knew his music.

"Well that's because I'm funny, " I was crossing my eyes and chomping down hard at each syllable. A couple more moments of laughter then I had to regain my composure. I shook my head and when the shaking was through, my normal, everyday face was back. A story-teller must remain professional, after all. "Know what's not funny?" I asked.

"Black eyes?" with the same emphasis I had given earlier.

Casting a wink his way I carried on. I slouched down in the couch cushions that now served as my driver's seat comparison. I looked down to the two empty spots to my right on the couch. I moved my left arm up and down from the rest to my thigh. Lucas looked curiously at me with one good eye. After deeming the couch too large for a proper demonstration I asked the kid to swap me the smaller loveseat for the deluxe model and the coveted "Dad Spot" to boot.

I sat on the left side of the smaller sofa and placed my arm on the armrest. "This works better." I nodded. Slouching again with my right leg straight and my toes pointed as hard as I could, I picked up the story.

"So say this loveseat is the front of my trashed car." I broke position and acted out as if, in slow motion, this deer bursting through. *You're in the jungle!* Slow motion facial reaction and mouthing the words "What the" and the forbidden *F-bomb*. Then followed by a sad excuse to block a Mike Tyson punching, antler head-banging, screaming in distressed Deer-tongue language of yore, beastly bastard.

"Caught up?" I asked my giggling spawn.

"Yeah. Deer on your lap kicking your butt worse than I do in football."

21

"Funny. Yes, so there I am with this deer hoofing me and—" Lucas halted me.

"Dad? Is it hoofs or hooves?" The ice pack slowly lowered from his now definite black eye. The first word came out sounding rushed and like *huffs* and the seconds *who-oves*, almost questioningly. I repeated both variations aloud six or seven times before coming up with the only logical answer I could in Dad-like speed.

"Hoofs. That's how us city people say it. Hoofs. It's those hilljack country folk that say 'Hooves', scoffing and allowing the vowels to linger a moment more before finishing the word. "Hooves. Just doesn't sound the same." Shaking my head I asked, "May I continue, Punk?" A smirk and a nod shot in my direction.

"I'm twenty five back then so I'm obviously not as *dad-bodded* out as I sit slouched before you, Son," his little laugh caught that moment in between my words and me refilling my lungs with more air grew an instant smile on my mouth. "So I'm a little bit tougher then than now, that's what I'm getting at." My left arm now swinging steadily back and forth rather than frantically as it had been on the couch, not the focal point as the tale of the hoofs went on.

"Onward and upward we go. So I am catching less-and-less blows to my face, neck, and collarbone area because I'm blocking them a little more-and-more. And that's not the only thing I am doing more-and-more of, either."

"What else was more-and-more?"

I started sawing up and down on my right leg at a pace matching my blocking left arm and asked, "What do I always carry on me? Same as Papa used to and like all my brothers do and your brother and you?"

Bolting up like an airbag had gone off underneath the poor lad, Lucas exclaimed, "Your pocket knife!"

"You're damn right my pocket knife." Cool, calm, collected, and in total adoration of my son like I was the smartest person alive for carrying a basic twenty dollar foldable knife. But therein lies the problem at hand. "I had a knife. Game over, right?" Lucas nodded twice and then began to shake his head and, eventually, shrugged his shoulders in unknowing fashion. "Game definitely not over?"

"I had a pocket knife. That was it. I didn't have a deer rifle. Sure as shit didn't have a deer shotgun. No crossbow out of nowhere in my pocket. A basic three inch steel blade that had cut down more cardboard boxes at my dumb job back when I was stuck in my Pontiac than it had slayed the magic flying deer that just so happened to stage dive into my private rock concert."

The excitement was back in my performance and Lucas was, once again, finding that sweet spot that lay hidden on the reverse of the 'green peas on white plastic bag' brand of swell-repellent that we were using to stop the swelling. The time spent in the backyard tossing the ball back and forth just being *us* long forgotten as his attention was solely devoted on Mr. Quarterback turned to Mr. Oh Shit a Deer.

"Battling away at getting the knife out of my pocket and the top of my blue jeans, I finally managed to get the damn thing loose and in my weakened grip. Hooray, right? Stab, stab, Dad's out?" I looked at Lucas who was slowly turning his head to the left then right. He didn't answer me back, just let his smile turn into a smirk that made me smile. That fake sinister grin he made washed clean off that mug of his as his smile took over. Again showing the need to improve his poker face delay.

"You're damn right no," again, faking enthusiasm as the original finding of the knife itself. "I still had what felt like my weight now as compared to then on my lap. Bambi, in the flesh. Er, fur," I corrected and continued. "What the hell am I supposed to do? Let this deer pummel my beautiful pre-"you turned me old" face? Let this thing knock me out cold? Kick me to death in my car? Figure out how to bring its hind legs in and either catapult his stuck ass across me and my spot in this car or, worse, uses four god-damn hoofs and kicks the shit out of not only me but the passenger seat and side of my piece of crap four door at the same time as I hold onto a Walmart pocket knife that would take me literally forever to kill a deer with like some sort of jackass?"

I was stringing together sentences and words so fast that Lucas had taken the bag of peas off of his face and was holding it with white knuckle grip in both hands—firmly planted on his lap with delight— as his Dad was telling him the greatest story he had heard in his eleven years on this deer infested world.

JASON MYERS

The tone in my voice went from playful and joking to a darker vibe. My son, the kid who is about to have an entire classroom of kids asking him what happened. My child, the one who would eat up the attention to come, walking around school with a black eye and be in absolute bliss with all non-swollen eyes on him. My son, Lucas, blurted out "Oh crap! Dad's about to get messy!" His little hands clapped tight together at the palms as his fingertips on one hand tapped against the other in classic Charades for *sinister*. "Aren't ya', Dad?"

"You're damn right I am, bud."

"I took another, like, fifteen hoofs to the face and then the side of it by the time I reached that fucking knife," no muffling of it that time. "You've seen those fighting pay-per-views enough to know that taking that many shots to the chops is a death sentence. Son, women are right when they say men are hard headed because that furry shithead was doing his best to end me right there. Fifteen hoofs, but I had the knife. And my left arm."

"Lucas? What hand do you write with?"

"Left," he answered.

"Throw with?" I asked him with one eyebrow up. Encouraging his mind to figure out where this was headed before asking, "Flick your nasty boogers with?" The playfulness back for just that question as Lucas's brain understood exactly where this was going, afterall.

"Punch with? Stab a wild animal to death with? With such a horrible weapon of all things. You, boy, are left handed. Where I," a pause to enhance the now obvious conclusion that, "I am right. Why don't you try and use that weak right arm of yours," I shrugged my still fake-trapped right shoulder, "And stab old Blitzen a few hundred times."

"Is that what you did?" Lucas asked. The fluttering in his eyelid finished and the sad aftermath of an all too familiar backyard accident sat across from me. Planted there for days to come.

"Twelve" I stared at Lucas as I repeated the number, blinked, and said,"I stabbed that deer a dozen times with a shitty little three inch knife. Somewhere about stab number eighteen or so," I was making a wishy-washy, back and forth motion with my left hand, "That's when that buck moved enough that I could somehow wrench my right arm free from it."

In unison with the words, I *wrenched* my right arm free from the *deer* I had just prison shanked with a very ironically branded Buck knife. I made a motion and the *knife* was now in my dominant grip and strength. Lucas followed my acting and talking out the fight of my life without missing a single syllable. His right eye followed the imaginary weapon move hand to hand—his left eye too closed to track it.

"Now. Now was the time when things felt like they were at a crawl. That 'slow-mo' feeling was here to stay and play as I blocked with my left forearm and stuck that poor deer that many times."

Lucas interjected at my use of the word. "Poor deer? Screw the deer. Poor you, Dad!"

"No, no." I pleaded to him. "Poor him. He was just cruising along too. I was on the

31

way to my girl and he was on the way to his. Accidents happen. This one just really sucked because now I have to tell you about it all because of *that* black eye." I pointed to his face and then to the thawing bag of peas. "Yeah, that is going to be fun explaining to your mother. Put the bag back on. I can get the frozen veggies if you need to switch out."

"That's okay. This one is still okay and my eye doesn't even really hurt now. More numb than anything."

I laughed and said, "Weird how that works, huh?" I quickly flashed the same goofy, chomping face as earlier and said, "Well keep it on there until I'm done with the 'Hoofs' story, at least. Okay? *Lucky*?" Another laugh. "I mean, Lucas."

"*Hoofs*. Not *Hooves*." No longer a question but a simple statement, Lucas urged me to proceed. "You stabbed a deer twelve times. Go, go."

"So," taking the last of the coffee slowly, then continuing, "Out of the twelve 'stabs'," setting down my cup and making air-quotes with my hands,"I think I managed to puncture that tough hide of his twice. The other times it more or less bounced off of it and *bam, bam* hoofs. Right to the face. I'd try and stick it again. *Bam, bam.* More hoofs."

B ack to playing couch charades with my kid eating up the story. Frozen peas left to thaw on the floor now, between his feet. Lucas was perched on the toes of his feet, his elbows touching his thighs. His hands were together at the palms under his chin holding the weight of his young head by it. The black eye was prominent and I knew that another hoof-like verbal beating was headed my way in a red minivan to pick up our son and take him back to their house for the week at school. His Monday was going to be epic as he is king of the mountain in recess-cred.

My Sunday evening to come was shit that rolls down that mountain. The dreaded "This crap always happens on your watch. Do you realize this?" talk. The "Typical. Just fucking typical" moment that every man dreads knowing that — to really no fault of his own, — your shared time happens to always play host to the injuries and accidents that are bound to happen in growing kids. The scolding-to-be by the one, the only, the ex-wife.

"So I am still totally pinned beneath Rambo-Bambi who is now finally running out of steam with the ferocity of its instinct in nature *hoofing* of me. I cut this poor," pausing to look at Lucas and make a sad face that would have impressed any mime who watched, "Poor deer and one of them, yes, did nic its jugular."

At that moment I pretended to puncture the imaginary animal on my lap's neck with my very real pocket knife. Lucas fell back the eight or so inches it took to land with his back against the couch, bending only at the waist. His legs never budged. "Poor deer." Lucas nodded and I did the same. That exact moment, I knew what I had to do with the retelling of "Hoofs" misadventure to my shiner sporting son.

We nodded in agreement that what I had done so many years prior in the inside of a shitty little Pontiac in the living room that my child— my almost teenage child— heard the 'almost teenage child' version of my "deer ass whooping" turned "I did what I had to do, fight for my life" saga.

Fifteen minutes of "Hoofs" and as I was wrapping it up in dramatic fashion, the hopefully understanding mother of my child was texting me that she would be there in just a few minutes. I read the text on my phone as it popped up and replied, sat the phone back on the loveseat and stood, stretching my arms high above me as I did.

"Mom just texted. She's almost here. I'll get the peas, you go get your stuff."

"Thanks, Dad. I will never forget that. Hoofs." Lucas was picking up the unfrozen peas off of the floor then looked at me and winked. "Not 'hooves'." And with that he was rushing through my house grabbing his things and I was headed to the kitchen for another cup of coffee.

The coffee pot was empty so I went through the process of making an entire pot of it, cursing myself aloud as I did about needing to *Just break down and buy a K-pod one.* When my awaiting cup was finally full of the deliciousness, my ex, Angela, walked into my house, announcing that she was there in the process.

"Lucas, I'm here bud. Got your stuff?" she called to the back of my door as she closed it behind her.

"Hey, uh, there was a little accident just a bit ago," I began as my ex-wife turned around to see me instead of our son.

"Typical. Just fucking typical." I heard her say it with my eyes closed and nodded as she tore into me. All in all, she was more upset when he broke his leg on the trampoline at Easter which she kindly threw in my face.

Then Mr. All-star with the black eye to disprove it came pouncing down the stairs, skipping the last three altogether.

"Oh. My. Lord." Just three words was all I let her get out. Then it was the insta-snap of her neck in my direction that sent them home and goosebumps to my flesh as I quickly interjected.

"It was an accident. Sorry again 'Lucky'." He walked casually over to me and gave me a hug.

"Look at it now, Dad. It will be gone in a couple of days like you said." Lucas pointed at the black eye and smiled. "At least it is just one eye and not *eyes*." The smile turned into a laugh and another quick hug before he turned to his mother. "Did Dad ever tell you his 'Hoofs' story?"

"Hooves. It's pronounced hooves," Angela corrected me matter of factly.

I lost myself laughing along with Lucas before he added sarcastically, "Either way it was super gross and funny. Thanks Dad." Lucas put his weekend overnight backpack on and was out the door to get into his mother's van. When he was clear of earshot, my ex-wife glared hard into my soul, scaring me quite frankly.

"Super gross and funny? What the fuck does that mean? He is eleven. Don't tell him super gross stories."

I shook my head and headed to sit back down on the loveseat that served as my old dead Grand Am to enjoy my coffee. "I told you about that deer that burst through my car and pinned me down before didn't I?"

JASON MYERS

Scoffing, she answered me, "No. I don't remember that one. If it's so gross why did you tell him? I know how nasty you get when you start parading around and acting out your stories. Use your head."

"Hoofs. Hooves. Whatever. I watered it down," I said calm and reassuringly. "I gave him the appropriate amount of blood, nuts, and guts." I had both of my arms in front of me, index fingers extended while all the other digits were tucked away. Mockingly I was waving my arms in a sing-songy fashion that I knew would both piss her off and make me laugh at the same time. Shot taken, shot landed.

I asked her if she wanted a coffee or anything and she politely declined. Though we may have made an awful couple in a relationship stance, we always managed to get along and co-parent with the best of them since the divorce. Years of adjusting schedules and years of moving on, when the proverbial dust had settled and bygones were bygones, we were just Lucas' parents. And in the grand scheme of things, everyone is better off for it.

I looked out the front windows and saw our son, football in hand, slow motion re-acting to his ball nailing him in the eye. Then he would take a fast step backward, reset position, and do the ball to the eye act again. After the third time he flinched and looked to spot me staring at him. His true intention revealed in that oversized smile plastered on his freckled face. I smiled as I pointed to him then mimed out laughing in an over-acting fashion—my shoulders clear up to the tops of my ears before pulling them down. The classic "Ha ha, that's what you get" laugh that every father masters by the time their child is a toddler.

"Growing pains" my mind flashed with nostalgia from the phrase. Time and time again, my late father would chalk up any accident as 'growing pains'. Hook your own finger putting bait on your hook? Growing pains. Twist your ankle showing off shooting hoops in the driveway? Growing pains. Football to the eye because you were showing off?

"Growing pains," I said outloud and in the best impression of my dad I could do. "He will be okay. Hell, I could have told him the story about knocking myself out cold with an aluminum baseball bat hitting rotten crab apples in the yard. Tossed one up, swing, *ping*. Lights out. About his age too actually."

Angela motioned with her right hand circling the air to 'get on with it' and I turned away from looking out the window and now toward her.

"He slanted and then tried to catch the football with one hand, diving like a bonehead at the same time, and the ball locked onto his left baby blue like a heat seeking missile and," I raised my palms upward chest level in front of me shrugged my shoulders in normal 'up to chin' height. I grabbed my coffee and took another drink as she sat where Lucas had been when I told him the same thing I was about to repeat to her.

She looked me dead in the eyes with the straightest lips and stern look on her eyebrows as she shook the frustration and her

45

head at the same time and said, "Dumbass. The gross shit. I'm intrigued."

Never one to turn down a chance at telling a story to any persons asking, I proceeded to tell her the same version of "Hoofs" — she shuddered every time I used that term in lieu of the grammatically correct, be it less fun, word *hooves*— leaving off the ending in a PG-13, pushing hardcore at R rated, tale of how I got the worst pair of black eyes in my life.

"Super gross and funny," nodding this time rather than shaking in disapproval as was par for most courses, "I guess I can give the kid that. Now spill it."

"Ope," I exclaimed. "Nice choice of words there Mom. Did I not just 'spill it' enough for you? Was there not enough bloodshed and poor deer," the air quotes

46

driving back the point that I had made just prior to Lucas and a point that his mother was on my side with.

The deer was a "poor deer" and didn't deserve its final moments alive being stuck inside of my car with the most iconic debut song by any band in recollection blaring at full volume. Maxed out with Slash soloing away and me, covered in what was running through his veins as they slowly leaked on me. Slowly, that was, until that dam let loose and the floodgates were opening. All this time, I was screaming like a tornado siren in storm season in between hoof after hoof of the beatdown was over.

"Poor deer. He deserved better. For that day, I am sorry." I nodded to her and asked one final time before continuing on with the tale I named "Hoofs" many years ago.

"Are you sure you want to hear the nasty shit I had to do that day to get out of that stupid car? Because if not, so be it. The ending is still the same as you just heard. The middle is just a smidge different from what Little 'Lucky' Lucas got to hear."

Assuring her as I walked back into my house with a few nods that Lucas was fine and talking to his buddy on the phone about his growing pain, I took my place back on the loveseat. No longer slouching and climbing all over it in dramatic fashion, I sat down and glanced at the steam coming off the rim of my black coffee mug.

"You refilled me?" I asked and she nodded. "Thanks, much appreciated."

"No worries. I filled it when I grabbed a water out of the fridge. Sorry but I'm not

JASON MYERS

sorry because I peeked at your freezer se-
lection while I was looking for an ice pack
for our son. You used peas, didn't you?"

Proudly, "Damn straight I did."

"Where's the ice pack? I want to get one
on it for the ride home."

"Relax, *Mom*. It's as down as the
swelling is going to be by now. If for
whatever reason it should swell up again,"
mocking jazz-hands in front of me, "Get
your own damn frozen peas out of your
freezer." I played back to her.

"So," She took a deep breath and closed
her eyes. "So what really happened inside
of that car with that deer?" It wasn't until
after asking that she opened her eyes, fully
prepared to hear what I had omitted from
Lucas' story.

"So the deer definitely did come bursting through my car and did get stuck," I began reassuringly. "I just kind of, maybe told him the version where I 'stabbed the deer and waited for help to arrive' at the end of it." She rolled her eyes and sat back into the cushions, knowing full well after all these years in each other's lives that it wasn't "the end".

"Well?" Angela smiled thesmile that had drawn me to her so many years ago. Genuine in delivery and in full anticipation of my retelling.

"Well alright, you twisted my arm," I joked back from the opposite couch. "Be prepared and get comfortable as I tell you the *actual* tale of 'Hoofs'."

"It's pronounced 'hooves'. Moron."

"Listen here," pointing a playful finger towards my ex-wife. "The next time you get bombarded with a white tail through your soccer mom mobile parked out there," I now pointed at the red minivan that sat behind my vehicle in the driveway, "You can call your story 'Hooves' if that *behooves* you," shooting her a wink as I let the pun land home.

"But until that time, I must warn you now that the graphic nature of what I am about to tell you is far beyond the normal nasty and spooky things I have told you prior to today. I urge that if you are squeamish or don't want to hear about blood, antlers, shit, and vomit— then perhaps the version I gave Lucas would hold you over?"

Taking the warning for what was about to be shared seriously, my son's mother closed her eyes and nodded her head slowly. "Tell me the gross 'Hoofs'."

Proceed with caution. Dead deer ahead.

I cleared my throat and began the Storyteller's Prefered Edition of 'Hoofs', repositioning myself to the stuck position I was left in before.

"So I'm doing everything I can to work up enough damn strength in my left arm from that stupid little seat I was stuck in. This fucking monster was cut on his jugular and still stomping my face the whole time. When I kept slashing away I realized then that it wasn't his artery that I had cut that I saw all the blood leaking from. It was from just above one of his," I stopped before finishing the sentence. I looked across the car-couch I was once again pinned inside of. I raised one eyebrow and waited for her to finish it for me.

"His *hoofs*. God I feel disgusting just saying that hilljack word of yours," she said and smiled, shaking her head back and forth twice as she did.

Clicking my tongue and aiming a finger pistol to her, assuring her that she was correct, I agreed. "His fucking hoofs. I thought I got him in the widowmaker but, alas, it was merely a deep gash on his wrist?" I ended the sentence aloud to her as a question, the same as I had done with Lucas before she arrived. I pointed at my right arm directly at one of my tattoos. "Right about here, where this little dinosaur is tatted." I tapped on Spike, my pet dinosaur tattoo and then quickly burst all my fingers wide open.

"All of that exploding crimson blood so fucking fast, girl, I tell you. I thought that I got him right then. Bam. Done. I was ready to close my eyes and just wait for this big son of a bitch to bleed out all over me. I knew that was what would happen. I knew it was him or me. Either I was going to stick his Bambi ass or he was gonna hoof me to death in my Pontiac."

"This thing is pissed. His grunts went from a 'panic that he was trapped and doing everything he could to break free' to more of a roar and 'I am going to stomp your mother fucking windpipe shut, stupid asshole human. Any second now and then while you gasp for air I'm going to bring one half of

these antlers inside of here one way or another and stab you repeatedly.'

Angela's turn to stop me in place. She
had both of her hands up in a classic stop
position and was pumping the air in front
of them. "Without all the F-Bombs please.
Grow up."

"What the fuck is an F-bomb? Ope, just
kidding. Yes, yes. Onward?" I asked her.
She nodded knowing she would always win
small battles like that. As a co-parent, I have
learned that as long as the mother of your
child is mad at other people in the world and
you are doing your end of the work, it is best
to just go along with whatever she wants.
She's going to get her way in the end so don't
delay the inevitable.

"Onward. I keep stabbing at him and doing my best to block the hoof-makers that

he was raining down on me. The more exhausted I was getting the more wound up this deer would get. My big prediction from before was coming true and the tip of one of that buck's points was scratching at the headliner of my car with authority."

I began wrenching my neck to the right in my best Regan ala Exorcist and rested it on my shoulder. I went from looking at my ex to staring directly at the ceiling of my living room that was housing the interior of my Pontiac. My left hand was still clutching the pocket knife that I held in my nondominant hand. "It was about six inches inside the window, dragging slowly and first breaking the thing that you push and it *pops*—making the noise as I said it—open and I store my shades in."

"Your sunglasses holder?" Angela asked snarkily, knowing damn well that it was, in fact, technically called a sunglasses holder. But, '*pop*, shade storage' was a close fill in.

I snapped and said, "Yeah, that's it. Well it broke and cut through that like I was slicing bread. That's some hard ass plastic in that old car. I knew that if he bucked down hard enough, he was going to royally F-bomb me up."

My ex-wife, the quick witted one she is said, "Fuck that's terrifying." A quick laugh escaped her lips before smirking back at me.

"Oh sure, you get to say it and I'm stuck with freaking F-bombs. But," I turned my hands over in acceptance that Mama was happy and therefore, I was too, "Yeah. It was fucking terrifying, alright." Back to the starting position I went, slumping down on the love seat. Trapped and clutching my knife in my left hand, the blade closed long after I wrapped up the version I told Lucas.

"Bleeding all over me from his hoof," I side eyed her, almost daring her to correct me again, "And it was still just beating the ever loving shit out of me at the same time. I knew it then as I tell you now, I had about one minute, maybe two," I wiggled the knife hand back and forth, "Give or take, doesn't matter. I had less than two minutes of fight in me before I accepted being hoof'd to death slowly or, worse, impaled and decapitated by this poor animal."

Patience is always a virtue in life. Another lesson I've learned as a co-parent dad. Take the time to tell the stories that your kids ask about. Really dig in and give it your all. They are, afterall, giving up precious screen time on the devices that we parent's allow them to abuse, just to hear you tell it. Patience and I noticed then, Angela staring at me, angrily.

As I slouched further still into the seat cushions, I was reminded with one interjection from Angela to, "Hurry the fuck up, our child is in the van and I need to get an actual icepack on his blackeye pronto. I thought you were the '*short* story guy'?"

I sat up and crossed my leg back over my knee, angling myself to her as I grabbed the coffee she had so kindly poured me. Sipping slowly on the black cup I held now in my left hand in lieu of the knife that I replaced back into my blue jeans, I continued the story.

"Alright, moving along. I ended up hitting my elbow down on the two buttons that roll down the rear windows as I was trying to reposition that sorry excuse for a knife. That spooked the absolute shit out of that thing."

"Literally?" Angela shot out.

"No, no. Not literally. It scared it enough that it did manage to bring one of its hind legs in through the front window," I pointed with my right index finger to the left, "Back between the space on the right of the passenger seat and back shotgun riders slide in," pointing the same finger directly back at myself now.

"And when a deer crashes your fucking door," blocking and muffling my mouth with my coffee mug like I had done for my son's retelling, I tucked my index finger into my palm in a flash and stuck my thumb out and to the right in just as much a hurry, "Some jackass opens a window."

"Poor jackass." Angela, right on cue, with that same smile.

"This poor *deer*," I emphasized, "Was trying to push off the inside of my car like we used to do as kids growing up in swimming pools with one leg and I was afraid if he brought the other one in with it, that it was going to shred me as it went breaking on through to the other side as Jim Morrison said. A few more pulses on my lap from the deer and I heard the free leg scratching metal with a fury, dying to come in."

I finished off the coffee and sat the empty cup on the coaster to my left. Nodding again in thanks to Angela for it. "So I used every last bit of energy I had right then inside of me and threw a fastball style left arm down like the slasher films of olde. As the blade was making an entry now, this deer had already twisted around a bit, and I missed his neck altogether." I leaned a little to my right and used my left index finger to first touch, just below my left nipple, and then drew a jagged line, like a series of lightning bolts, across my stomach and down to just below my navel.

"I kept it in this time. I didn't have it in me to keep just poking around at him with a dull pocket blade. His other hoof breached the frame of my car and he was, as I feared, about to push off and, pending some sort of miracle, that furry fucker makes it across with just one push? What are the odds of that?" I didn't give her a chance to answer.

"Not good. That's what they are," I answered myself. "Deer, oh deer, was probably going to get halfway in and push off, cock his stupid fucking head all awkward and twisted up. Break through the windshield. Actually cut his jugular on that. Push off again. This time using *me* as the springboard. Then, those sharp as all hell hoofs."

"Hooves. I can't stand you sometimes. Just say it right. *Hooves*."

"I most certainly will not." I shot snarky and playfully in unison. "Those sharp as hell hoofs were going to cut me to my death in my driver's seat. I plunged that cheap ass knife into that deer and pushed up so hard," I was clenching down my left hand into a fist in front of my chest so hard that it began shaking in place, "And that thing pole vaulted across and I just held the knife in as deep as I could as it went."

"I pushed so damn hard, Angela, that," I moved my right hand, open faced, and smashed it into my left fist. Holding it there, the side of my left pinky against the heel of my right hand, I rolled it over. My knuckles now facing me on my left hand, I pushed it through my right.

"You put your hand in?" Angela asked.

"Not my whole hand," I nodded, "But enough that it helped in getting enough ass behind the blade to gut that poor deer and stop it in place, open wound just pouring out the absolute foulest smelling red and brown and orangish mixed-color nasty shit all over me. I'm there screaming my young head off and that is the last thing that creature got to hear. Me. Screaming—likely crying—as his life flows out of it in teeny. Tiny. Little. *Spurts*. Every five seconds or so"

"*Spurt*," I flashed my left hand and drug imaginary vital necessities out of the make believe deer with my right. "*Spurt*," Again the same gesture. "*Spurt*," repeated a third time. "You get it. That deer would spasm and pop out a good section of intestines and the rest of what was in there. Then drip all over my chest and lap. Spasm and more would seep out. Three nasty fucking times that thing went *spurt*," a final gesture to push it over Angela's already tested limits.

"Then I felt the final hoof of its life nail me right in the damn eye a last time. A final 'hoof in my coffin', if you will? And it died. Right there. I had about four solid seconds of relief before the realization came to me. Just because the deer isn't hammerfisting the absolute dogshit out of me doesn't mean I'm home free. I still had to get out of this blood mobile and to do that I needed to get out from underneath the wild whitetail on top of my pinned down lower half."

"Well, what did you do?" Angela asked the obvious questions. "How the hell did you get out?"

I smiled at her, satisfied that I had her attention and was preparing myself for the gruesome points that I restricted myself from giving our preteen son. "I died. Right there in my driver's seat."

Scoffing at me, my ex responded, "Jackass. Obviously you didn't die. You're here wasting my time and testing my damn patience.

How did you get out? A passerby? The girl you were meeting?"

I was shaking my head slowly and followed up with, "I got out of that car the same way I came into this world, Angela. Screaming, crying, scared to death, and covered in someone else's blood. Well, maybe not someone, but clearly something." I smiled after I said it, waiting for her reaction. She simply sat on her couch, crossed her arms, and waited for me to continue with one eyebrow raised.

"So I managed to gut the first and only deer I have killed in my life. A hunter can go years without bagging a buck. And all it took me was a late model Pontiac and horrible fucking timing. Chasing after tail and the wrong one lands in my car. The part that I sliced open on its stomach was leaking like a dam and the smaller slitI had cut into his neck was just trickling slowly. I was caked and coated in the shit." I raised my index finger from my seated and smashed position on the loveseat under the windows, the sun setting into the flat land that is Ohio. An important side note was in order and a better segway could never present itself as it just did.

"Did you know, dear Angela," I began.

She stopped me with a matching finger. "Dear or deer?" Her emphasis on the animal variation of the word. One thing for certain, our son Lucas was bound and determined to be a quick witted smart ass like both of his parents.

"Dear, as in 'Oh, dear, you're funny.'" I puckered my mouth into a small O and squinted my eyes in an attempt to scrunch my whole face. Angela smiled, knowing that her cleverness was a shot taken and shot landed for herself. Then, as quickly as I made the face, she returned it right back.

"Deer, much like us human counterparts, void their bowels upon death. So, follow along with me. I stab," making the motion with my left hand, "barely doing damage. Stab, stab, stab. Hoof, hoof, hoof." Still blocking the onslaught of hoof beats. "And this sloppy, heavy, son of a bitch lets loose all of the wonderful wilderness treats of berries, apples, and Lord knows what else all over my fucking shotgun seat."

In my replaying of the scene, I sat pressed down on the couch cushions, slow motion revisiting the startled look in my face, pretending to watch a dead two hundred pound deer let loose a water cannon expul-

sion of scat and shit all over my make believe sofa. Acting as though I was truly
trapped and fighting for my life, I began
panicking and trying to cover my nose
comically.

"You're an idiot." One small laugh from
Angela as I carried on.

"I really wish I was making that part
up," I apologized. "But old Bambi did add
smeary shit into the color palette interior
options that I don't believe GM offered
back in the day. So I'm freaking out royally because, again, poor deer." I lowered
my head in an apologetic motion, still
saddened to this day about the unfortu-
nate events that took place in the middle
of the country road I sat idling on. "That
big nasty deer was matted in spilling blood
and excrement and, now, so was I."

"Trying to breathe inside my sedan was like taking in a hot shower fart. No matter what you do, it just seems to always hover about, right near your nostrils."

"It's amazing I ever gave you a chance. You know that, right?" Angela chuckled.

"Yeah, yeah. Lucky me. So, all shower stinks aside," I laughed and regained myself, "I really was in full on panic mode. Fighting for survival, I was a younger version of myself. Years of vast knowledge and experience I was lacking. Frantic yelling and shoving what felt like an immovable object until my strength was gone, now that was my bread and butter." Back to making exaggerated movements from the love seat, my left arm managed to sneak its way in the spot between couch cushions. Once I stopped jerking my shoulder and trying to pull my arm free, I looked at Angela and cast her a wink.

"With all the wiggling and twisting I had done, the once dying, and now dead, deer had rolled and freaked out just as much. So now I have since dropped the knife into the vast no man's land that seems to eat up all my lighters that fall out of my pocket. The knife had probably slipped down and under my driver's seat by now, but it was okay. The hard part was done."

My left hand triumphantly pulled itself out of the couch and instead of the cheap blade, I was simply exposing an extended index finger. "Voila!"

"Voila my ass," Angela made a fake choking noise as she interrupted me, "That finger has never been worthy of a 'voila'. More of a 'voi-meh'," a frown on her face as she exploded with her cackling.

"Whenever you are done attacking my masculinity as well as my prowess, let me know and I'll be happy to continue." Snidely I responded, smiling the whole while.

"Proceed valiant deer slayer. Onward with 'Hooves'." An instant correction as she rolled her eyes and said, "Or 'Hoofs', you weirdo."

"Hoofs, indeed." I closed my left hand, sans for the newly attacked digit that I left pointing toward the ceiling, "And voila, indeed, as well. A lot has changed since you and I were 'You and I', ya know?" Slowly, I stopped pointing at the sky and down towards my left thigh. I raised my eyebrows simultaneously three times in hope that Angela knew where I was headed with the explanation. The bewildered look on her face told me that more explaining was in order.

"Stupid Me found the window roll down buttons with my elbow. Smart Me, however, remembered the recline function on the side panel of my seat. Voi-fucking-la. My eyes were all but swollen shut, my nose blood mixing in with deer blood. I could taste the coppery taste of it all mixing into my opened mouth. I knew it then that my nose was broken. It felt exactly as it had when it got smashed up playing football just a few years prior in highschool. Dead buck, bleeding out all of his nasty life juice on my lap and just all fucking over my car. And me, sitting shakily as the seat I was taking up realty in slowly," looking directly at my ex wife, never losing her eye contact, "And I mean *slowly,* the seat reclined."

Eyes locked with Angela's, I methodically lowered myself into an almost laying position on the sofa—never blinking in my delivery. I added a *vrrrrr* sound and held the note it made as it left my mouth. "Voila. I now had some real wiggle room to make my great escape."

"Wonderful," Angela said sarcastically, motioning with her right hand to hurry up.

"Yeah, it was. Except, I was spent. I had just used up all the strength I had in my arms battling this bastard over the last five minutes or so. I was holding him back against my dashboard with my right hand, my left was still pushing the down button on the controls with as much muster as I had in me. The dead deer's hoofs just kind of dangled in front of me, caressing me as it left this world. I was exhausted. Then the stereo kicked back in. Guns N Roses may have gotten me into this bloody mess, but it seemed as though the radio deejays had a different hero to help in my aid of getting out.

I raised my left hand from the trenches it was working down inside of the loveseat and exposed the heavy metal horns. Pinky up, ring and middle tucked by my thumb, and index finger out. "At my hour of darkness and wanting, the commercial was over and, I shit you not, the beginning riff to AC DC's "Thunderstruck" was like Popeye downing a can of green spinach. Thunder!" I followed up my exciting new information to Angela by giving her the absolute worst Brian Johnson impression I could give her and added the "ahh ahh ahh ahh" parts before she hit me with the 'hurry up hand' again.

"You know our son would eventually like to go home, right? So, what happened?" Angela questioned.

"Alright, alright. I hear you." I sat upright on my seat and left the theatrics as I did. "No more stops in Hoofville."

"Idiot."

Nodding in agreement, I prepared myself to regale her with the ending. Drinking the last of the now warm coffee she had given me, I cleared my throat and said, "Dead deer on my lap and AC DC in my ears, it was literally do or die time."

"When the button wouldn't lower me anymore and the seat was as flat as I could make it go, I made my move. Pressing down hard with my right foot I felt like I was trying to put it through the sheet metal underneath it. I remember it kept rubbing against and sometimes even directly down on the gas pedal. My left foot was still holding the brake firmly to the floor. I reached across the bloody fur that was still dripping entrails onto me and managed to get my left hand over to the gear shifter. I

83

slammed that bitch into park with enough ass behind it I was afraid I was going to break it off in the process. No longer worrying about taking off at full speed into one of the ditches that surround all country roads, it was time to use my legs."

"I reached my left hand up and was blindly grabbing away, trying to reach the opening of the rear driver's side, opened window. My hand and arm were both slippery and sticky from the mix of deer and my blood that it made actually grasping the window a chore. Finally, I was able to grip it and push off with my legs. I managed to move all of three inches." Knowing my ex the way I do, I shushed her before she could chime in. "I readjusted, regripped, rekicked off the floor and again, just managed to scooch a few measly inches. Like the jackass you take me for, the seatbelt was still latched." Unable to breeze past my phrasing this time, Angela slipped in a "jackass".

"So, slowly and carefully again I reached across this fucking dead animal and unclicked my belt with my left hand. Instant relief as I managed to slay the wicked seatbelt monster and was ready for another shot at freedom. Calculating my next move, I knew I had one shot left in me to get out from under him."

Angela leaned in, a smile painted nicely on her face, prepared to sit silently as I concluded my story.

"My right hand, God bless that previously useless extremity, was losing the battle at pushing the deer carcass and I knew in my head that if I went reaching for the window behind me, the deer was going to roll and land completely on me in a bloody mess as I tried to slide out. But what other choice did I have? The music inside the car urged me to "Fight, fight, fight for your life" as I was doing just that myself. "Shaking at the knees" belted out from the speakers as it was play by play calling out my movements in sync with the lyrics, The time for pausing was over. It was time for action."

"I did just that. The instant I let the deer roll off the dash by removing my right hand, I pushed off a final time— both feet together at the same time— as I grasped the window, this time with both hands. I pulled my legs up to my blood soaked t-shirt and felt the fur of the deceased beast brush against my exposed ankles. Knees into my chest now, I pushed down against that animal and felt it squish and cave into the force of me using it as a springboard."

"The horn on my Pontiac blasted out as I kicked off the deer a final time, slamming my Adidas into his caved in side and making their final stance in getting me out of the driver's seat. I swear I popped out of the back window faster than that fucking thing did coming in. But, like a twenty something newborn, out into the road I was born. Covered in so much nasty gunk, it actually splashed up from me when I landed on the dirt road. Dust and blood and hoof fur all in a puff of freedom. I sat there on the road with my knees in my chest and rocked back and forth for several seconds."

Looking at my coffee cup on the table to my side and remembering the sad fact that it was empty, I slapped both of my knees with my hands and stood up tall off of my loveseat. "When the shaking was over and the blood was moving back to the parts of my body that I needed to use to stand up, I assessed the damage."

Angela, following in the same knee slap and standing up fashion, scoffed again and said, "Access the damage? Deer? Dead. Car? Totaled. Face? Fucked." Ticking off the answers on her fingers as she went. "What damage could you possibly need to access?"

Walking towards the kitchen with my empty coffee cup in hand, I debated on refilling it and then chose to just sit it down on the counter. "Um, hello? I was still trying to meet up with that girl and possibly get to some hoofing of our own."

Angela reached the front door as I was coming out of the kitchen. As her hand reached to turn the doorknob, she let her fingers sit before turning it. "Well?"

"Well what?" I questioned.

"Well, what ended up happening between you and her?" my ex wife asked me.

I met Angela at the door and laughed as we both exited together. "She was the first person to roll up on me that day on the road."

"Oh no. Did she freak out?"

"You tell me how *you* would react. A guy you have dated like two times is supposed to stop over. He is late. You decide to go and look for him only to discover him two miles down the way from you. He's half leaning, half collapsing on the hood of his car. He is dripping with all the entrails of a dead deer. Clearly he is out of breath and don't forget, he was ugly crying. Would you freak the fuck out?"

"I'd have driven on and kicked road dust in your eyes."

I nodded and said, "Lucky for me you weren't her." Noticing Lucas in the front seat, still tossing the football lightly up to himself I shouted out, "Isn't that right, Lucky?"

Swollen eye and all, my son Lucas kept his spirits high and said, "My name isn't Lucky, it's Lucas. Don't go spreading that nickname around."

"I'll work on that, you work on catching footballs with your hands and not your dome. And listen to your mother when she gets you an actual ice pack." Lucas nodded with a smile beneath his black eye. With no warning, standing just outside of my ex's minivan, I made a hurt grunt noise like the deer in my story and dove through the rolled down window, stopping at my waist. I wrapped both my arms around my son and squeezed as hard as the small room we took up let me.

As I let go of our embrace, I accidently rubbed the left side of Lucas' face, directly against his swollen peeper. "Watch your hooves, Dad," Lucas joked.

"It's 'hoofs' son. Hoofs."

Agreeing as his mother started the van and placed it in reverse, Lucas called back to me, "Hoofs".

About the Author

Jason Myers (1983-) grew up in Northwest Ohio. Avid reader for years he put aside his dreams of writing to raise his children and focus on being an

EMT/Firefighter. The need to write never left and in 2019 he released his debut DECISIONS based off of his real life reoccurring nightmare.

The momentum picked up and he quickly was listed in the table of contents in several horror anthologies as well as several novellas of his own.

He currently resides in Northwest Ohio retired from ems/firefighting after 10 years with his city fire department in Maumee, Ohio.

Also By
Jason Myers

Decisions

Cupid

See No Evil

MetamorPHASES: Collected Short Fiction

https://linktr.ee/cloverpeakpublishing

Made in the USA
Coppell, TX
21 March 2024